001151910

Jackson County Library Se
Medford, OR 97501

D0447721

Pedal Power

DATE DUE			6 / 98
▮▮▮▮▮▮	▮▮▮▮▮		
JUL 22 98			
JUL 27 '00			
	WITHDRAWN		
	Damaged, Obsolete, or Surplus		
	Jackson County Library Services		
GAYLORD			PRINTED IN U.S.A.

OTHER YEARLING BOOKS YOU WILL ENJOY:

A GIFT FOR TÍA ROSA, *Karen T. Taha*
A GRAIN OF RICE, *Helena Clare Pittman*
MOLLY'S PILGRIM, *Barbara Cohen*
MAKE A WISH, MOLLY, *Barbara Cohen*
WRITE UP A STORM WITH THE POLK STREET SCHOOL,
Patricia Reilly Giff
COUNT YOUR MONEY WITH THE POLK STREET SCHOOL,
Patricia Reilly Giff
THE POSTCARD PEST, *Patricia Reilly Giff*
TURKEY TROUBLE, *Patricia Reilly Giff*
SHOW TIME AT THE POLK STREET SCHOOL,
Patricia Reilly Giff
LOOK OUT, WASHINGTON, D.C.!, *Patricia Reilly Giff*
NEXT STOP, NEW YORK CITY!, *Patricia Reilly Giff*
LET'S GO, PHILADELPHIA!, *Patricia Reilly Giff*
OH BOY, BOSTON!, *Patricia Reilly Giff*

Pedal Power

Judy Delton

Illustrated by Alan Tiegreen

A Yearling Book

JACKSON COUNTY LIBRARY SERVICES
MEDFORD OREGON 97501

Published by
Bantam Doubleday Dell Books for Young Readers
a division of
Bantam Doubleday Dell Publishing Group, Inc.
1540 Broadway
New York, New York 10036

If you purchased this book without a cover you should be aware that this book is stolen property. It was reported as "unsold and destroyed" to the publisher and neither the author nor the publisher has received any payment for this "stripped book."

Text copyright © 1998 by Judy Delton
Illustrations copyright © 1998 by Alan Tiegreen

All rights reserved. No part of this book may be reproduced or transmitted in any form or by any means, electronic or mechanical, including photocopying, recording, or by any information storage and retrieval system, without the written permission of the Publisher, except where permitted by law.

The trademarks Yearling® and Dell® are registered in the U.S. Patent and Trademark Office and in other countries.

Visit us on the Web! www.bdd.com
Educators and librarians, visit the BDD Teacher's
Resource Center at www.bdd.com/teachers

ISBN: 0-440-41336-2

Printed in the United States of America

June 1998

10 9 8 7 6 5 4 3 2 1

CWO

For Kim French, who dedicates so much
to the Pee Wees

Contents

CHAPTER 1

Geronimo!

"Hey, get out of the way, you guys! I'm coming down that slide backward!" yelled Roger White. He and some of the other Pee Wee Scouts were playing in the park.

"Not on your bike, you're not!" shouted Rachel Meyers.

But Roger was hauling his bike up the steps of the slide, dragging and banging it all the way.

"Is he crazy?" asked Molly Duff. "This

is even dumber than the stuff he usually does!"

Mary Beth Kelly groaned. She was Molly's best friend. All of the thirteen Pee Wee Scouts were friends. At least most of the time. And of course not always with Roger. They were in second grade, and every Tuesday afternoon after school they met in Mrs. Peters's basement for their Scout meeting. They told about their good deeds and played games and had treats. They earned new badges by learning something new or doing something good for others.

"Mrs. Peters should see him," said Mary Beth. "He'd be kicked out of Scouts for good!"

"I feel like going over to her house and getting her!" said Patty Baker, who had a twin brother in Scouts named Kenny.

"She should see this for herself. She doesn't know how crazy Roger really is!"

But no one wanted to leave. They wanted to see what Roger would do. No one ever had ridden a bike down the slide—backward *or* forward. Was it possible? It would take someone like Roger to find out.

Roger turned the bike around at the top of the slide. Then he climbed onto the seat, holding on to the handrails on the slide at the same time.

"Geronimo!" he shouted. "Here I go!"

But he didn't let go of the handrails.

"Scaredy-cat!" called Tim Noon. "I dare you! I double-dare you!"

"Roger," said Ashley Baker, who was the twins' cousin from California and a temporary Scout when she was visiting them. "Listen to me! Come down from there this minute. You're going to break all your bones, and your bike is going to be smashed to pieces!"

Roger looked at his bike. He did not seem worried about his bones.

"Sometimes it's braver to back down than it is to go ahead," Ashley went on.

But Roger didn't like the sound of the words *back down*. The only way he would back down would be on his bike, down the slide. Tim and Sonny Stone (whose mother was the assistant Scout leader) were calling him names like "yellow" and "baby," so he let go of one handrail.

"I'm warning you!" said Ashley. "You'll be sorry!"

That was the last straw for Roger. It sounded like something his teacher would say. Or his parents. So Roger let go of the other handrail. Everyone screamed as Roger's bike, with Roger on it, plummeted

4

backward down the slide and over the edge. Roger fell to the ground with a crash. Clouds of dust and dirt rose up around him. His bike was dented. Roger didn't move. Nothing moved. The Pee Wees stared.

"He's dead!" yelled Sonny. "Roger's dead!"

Even Rachel, who was usually very calm, looked shocked.

Molly wondered what to do. They shouldn't just stand around in an emergency! They were trained to be helpers. If Jody George and Kevin Moe were here, she thought, they would know what to do. They were smarter than the others and always did the right thing.

What if Roger is dead? Molly thought. No Pee Wee had ever died before. Would they have to wear black clothes and go to his funeral? Would people cry? Roger's fa-

ther certainly would. Roger had no mother. If he had one, she would probably cry too.

Well, someone had to do something. Who would it be? Finally Kenny walked up to what was left of Roger and his bike. Kenny bent over and gave Roger a kick. "Get up! We know you're just kidding. You're not really dead."

But Roger didn't move. "I don't think he's breathing!" said Kenny, who looked scared now.

Rachel walked over and joined him. She bent down and lifted a handlebar.

"He's bleeding!" she screamed. "Call 911!"

CHAPTER 2

Emergency!

"Get someone!" shouted Rachel. "Hurry! Call 911!"

Molly grabbed Mary Beth and the two girls ran out of the park to the first house they saw. They pounded on the door and shouted, "Emergency!" to the woman who opened it. "Call 911," they said. "Our . . . friend isn't breathing!"

The woman looked out into the park and saw the crowd gathered around Roger. She dialed the number. "They're sending someone right away," she said.

The woman ran back to the park with the girls. She brought a blanket and laid it over Roger and his bike. "It's best not to move anything," she said.

Before long, everyone could hear sirens.

"You know," said Mary Beth thoughtfully, "if Roger isn't dead, he still might be in the hospital a long time. He'd miss our Pee Wee meetings."

Molly thought of Pee Wee Scouts without Roger. No fighting. No throwing food. No smart remarks and insults. It would be easy not to miss Roger.

The sirens got closer. A fire engine, a police car, and an ambulance pulled up. Two policemen jumped out, followed by two women with a stretcher.

"They don't need that fire engine," said Sonny. "Roger's dead, he's not on fire!"

"I'm a paramedic," said one of the women. "Clear the way!" Everyone

9

stepped back, and the emergency team gathered around Roger. They pulled medical-looking things out of their first-aid box.

The medic shook her head.

"Uh-oh," said Ashley. "That doesn't look good."

"It could just mean she thinks Roger was really dumb to go down the slide on his bike," said Patty.

Soon Roger was on the stretcher and being wheeled into the ambulance.

"Don't worry about your friend," said a policeman to the Pee Wees. "They'll take good care of him. You can help us by answering a few questions."

The police asked for Roger's name and address. Then they said, "Did someone push him over the edge?"

The Pee Wees told them the whole story. Rachel added, "Sometimes I'd *like* to push him over the edge, but I'd never really do it."

After the police had left, Ashley said, "They were trying to see whether we murdered Roger. They must think his accident looks suspicious."

"They don't know we're Pee Wee Scouts," said Mary Beth. "Scouts don't hurt anyone. They help people."

"If we had murdered him we wouldn't call 911," said Tracy.

"We might," said Kenny. "I saw a mystery on TV where the murderer called the police so they wouldn't think it was him."

The Pee Wees didn't know what to do. This was a brand-new experience for them. It wasn't one they could get a badge for, but it was new just the same. And Mrs. Peters wasn't even there.

Molly thought it was strangely quiet in the park without Roger. The Pee Wees just stood around looking at his dented bike. Molly felt a little bit shaky, the way she had when she was in the Pee Wee talent show.

After a few minutes of silence, Tim said, "Well, I have to go home."

Slowly the others left as well. What else can we do? thought Molly.

"I think we should tell Mrs. Peters," said Mary Beth on the way home.

"And Roger's dad," said Ashley. "His dad should know he's . . . hurt."

"The police will tell him," said Kenny.

"Mrs. Peters might get too excited," said Molly. "She might blame us for not stopping him. I'm going to tell my mom when I get home, and she can call Mrs. Peters."

Everyone agreed that was a good idea.

"There you are!" said Mrs. Duff when Molly came in the door. "Your dad and I were beginning to wonder where you'd run off to. I told him you were probably just in the park having fun with your friends. Wash up for supper now, it's time to eat."

Molly went into the bathroom and washed her hands and face. She would save the bad news until later. It would ruin a perfectly good supper to report a dead Pee Wee.

At the table, Molly's dad ruffled her hair. Then he gave her a hug and said, "So what were you doing this afternoon— looking for trouble around town?"

Molly's dad liked to kid, but this time he was a little too close to the truth. Molly felt horrible. She couldn't keep quiet about Roger's accident any longer. She'd have to ruin the dinner, even though there were mashed potatoes and gravy. She loved mashed potatoes and gravy.

"Roger might be dead," she said. She was surprised to find tears running down her face.

Molly's parents stared at her. Her father's fork stopped in midair, and her mother held on, without moving, to the plate of pork chops she was passing. It's like a game of Statue Maker, thought Molly.

"He rode his bike down the slide in the park and went over the edge and crashed to the ground and there was some blood on him and he wasn't moving," Molly said in one big breath. "We called 911 and they took him away on a stretcher in an ambulance."

"Oh my," said Mrs. Duff, looking white. She set down the pork chops. Molly knew the food was getting cold, but she didn't care. She felt too sad to be hungry. Emergencies took a lot of energy.

"I'm sure he's okay," said Molly's dad.

"He didn't move and his eyes were closed," said Molly.

Mr. Duff stood up and walked toward the phone.

"Why don't you go to your room, Molly, while I make a few phone calls."

Just as Molly started upstairs, the phone rang. It was for Molly.

"He's okay," said Rachel in a disgusted voice. "He's just got a minor concussion. He's in the hospital."

"Oh. Thanks for letting me know," said Molly. "I'll see you tomorrow."

Molly felt relieved to hear the news. No matter how she felt about Roger, he was a Pee Wee Scout. He had done a dumb thing, but he didn't deserve to die for it.

"Roger isn't dead," reported Molly to her parents. "He has a concussion."

"Thank goodness," said Mr. Duff. "I

think I'll give his dad a call and see if there's anything we can do to help."

"Well, that is good news," said Molly's mother. "Let's finish our dinner while your dad gets the details."

Molly was glad to do that. Now that Roger was going to live, she could stop worrying. She put a large helping of potatoes and gravy on her plate, and two pork chops.

When her dad had finished his phone calls, he came to the table and said, "Well, it seems we have some heroes on our hands! The Pee Wees' fast thinking and calling 911 saved Roger's life."

CHAPTER 3

Heroes and Hospitals

The next day Mrs. Peters held an emergency Pee Wee meeting, even though it was only Monday.

"You can't imagine how pleased I was to find out that two of our own Pee Wees reacted promptly yesterday and saved Roger's life."

Rachel rolled her eyes at Molly.

"That's what being a Scout is all about: helping others," Mrs. Peters added. "And this was a life-or-death situation. I'm very proud. The police said if they hadn't been called so fast, Roger could have died."

Molly and Mary Beth turned bright red. The other Pee Wees clapped.

"Rachel thought of calling 911," said Molly. The Pee Wees clapped some more.

Mrs. Peters held up the morning paper. The headline said, "Scouts save local boy's life." The story that followed told how the two girls had run for help, and how the police and paramedics had come just in time.

"Hey, they should get a great big badge for saving my best friend's life," said Sonny. "Or maybe a medal."

"Saving his life is reward enough, I'm sure," said Mrs. Peters.

"As you all know," she went on, "Roger is in the hospital recovering from his accident. I thought we should all go and visit him. The doctor says he can have company for a short time."

"Mrs. Peters," said Ashley, "Roger's accident wasn't exactly an accident. He was fooling around with his bike on the slide."

Rachel and Molly and Mary Beth all nodded.

"My mom said he brought it on himself," said Mary Beth.

Mrs. Peters frowned. "Yes, I heard about that," she said. "And that's why tomorrow I'm going to tell you about our new badge. It's a badge that we all need to earn, and one that could save everyone's life. But right now it's time to go and cheer up Roger."

Mrs. Peters brought the van, and the Pee Wees piled in. When they got to the hospital they took the elevator to the third floor.

"It smells like medicine," said Sonny, holding his nose.

They did not have to look for Roger's room. They could hear him from all the way down the hall.

"I don't want soup!" Roger was shouting. "I want ice cream! The doctor told me I could have ice cream!"

A nurse came out of his room carrying a bowl of soup. She looked worn out. Her hair was all messed up and she was not smiling.

"I guess Roger hasn't changed any, even though he almost died," said Rachel.

"I thought he'd be nice now," said Mary Beth. "He should be grateful not to be dead."

When they went into Roger's room, Roger was acting far from dead. He was jumping up and down on the bed, demanding ice cream. He did not look

happy to see the Pee Wees. He just yelled, "Hey you guys, what did you bring me?"

Mrs. Peters looked as if she would like to yell at Roger. But all she said was "You'd better lie down and cover up. You could fall again, and this time you might not be so lucky."

The frazzled nurse returned with some ice cream in a dish.

Roger looked at it and shouted, "I want chocolate sauce on it!"

"If I was that nurse I'd throw it at him," said Mary Beth.

"She'd lose her job if she did that," said Tracy. "Nurses have to be nice to their patients."

When the nurse came back with the chocolate sauce, Roger screamed, "I want some nuts on it! Get me some nuts!"

This time Mrs. Peters walked up to Roger and talked to him in a low, stern voice. The Pee Wees heard her say the words *rude* and *unmannerly*. Roger frowned and ate the ice cream. He made loud smacking noises with his lips.

Mrs. Peters stepped out into the hall to talk to the nurse. Roger said, "Hey, Stone, press that button on the end of the bed!"

Sonny, who was glad to see his best friend again, pressed the button. The bed flew up on one end and down on the other. Sonny pressed it again, and the other end went up. All the boys wanted a turn pushing the button. All except Jody, who usually stayed clear of trouble. Besides, he couldn't reach the button from his wheelchair.

"Roger should be in jail instead of in the hospital," said Lisa.

"He's having so much fun, it's like he gets rewarded for doing dumb stuff," said Kevin.

"Mrs. Peters was wrong about us having to cheer Roger up," said Lisa.

"He's not even glad to see us," said Mary Beth. "And he didn't thank us for saving his life."

"I wouldn't be glad to see us either," said Ashley, "if I'd made such a fool of myself."

"Hey, Roger," said Jody. "You know what? In China, if someone saves your life you have to return the favor by taking care of them. If you were Chinese, you'd have to wait on Molly and Mary Beth all your life."

"Hey, I saw a movie about that on TV!" said Tim.

The boys started teasing Roger about waiting on Molly and Mary Beth.

"Hey, I'm not Chinese! Leave me alone! I'm not waiting on any old girls!"

"Good," said Mary Beth. "Because we

sure wouldn't want you hanging around us all the time."

"I think he should. It's the least he can do," muttered Ashley.

"I heard that if you don't repay the person for saving you," said Kenny, "you'll have bad luck for seven years. You have to do at least one good thing to pay them back."

Roger stopped what he was doing. "What kind of bad luck?" he asked Kenny.

"Oh, like if you got a new bike someone might come and steal it. Or you might get hit by lightning," he said.

"Maybe you'd get some awful disfiguring disease," said Rachel. "Or grow two heads or something."

"Steal my bike?" said Roger. "My new bike? My dad is getting me a new bike next week!"

Roger didn't seem to mind about the lightning, or having two heads.

Kenny nodded. "I think you better do something to repay them," he said. "I'd be scared not to."

Mrs. Peters came in again, followed by the doctor and nurse. The Pee Wees were asked to say good-bye and leave. The doctor gave Roger a look that said there would not be any more ice cream for him today.

"Well, I'm glad to see that Roger is improving," said Mrs. Peters when they were all in the van. "At least his concussion, I mean. It appears he's out of danger."

"If I was his dad, he'd be in plenty of danger," muttered Rachel.

Molly had to agree with Rachel. Somewhere inside, she was sorry she'd ever bothered to save Roger!

CHAPTER 4

A New Badge

The next day was Tuesday, and the Pee Wees gathered in Mrs. Peters's basement for their regular meeting. Roger was home from the hospital, but he wasn't able to go back to school yet—or to Pee Wee Scouts.

"I think we can all learn a lot from Roger's accident," said Mrs. Peters when all the Pee Wees were there. "Can you tell me one thing it taught us?"

Hands waved.

"You shouldn't ride down the slide backward on a bike," said Tim. "You can't see where you're going."

Mrs. Peters nodded. "Bikes have no business being on slides," she said. "Slides are not for bikes at all. Ever."

"I learned that hospital beds go up and down at the ends," said Sonny.

"And hospitals smell bad," said Tracy, holding her nose. All the Pee Wees held their noses and made faces.

"I learned something else," said Tim.

"Yes?" said Mrs. Peters, looking hopeful.

"Sometimes you bleed and you look dead but you aren't."

Mrs. Peters sighed. "Those are all important things," she said. "But I was thinking of something else. What can we learn about safety?"

"Don't fool around on the playground," said Kevin. "It can be real dangerous."

"That's right," said Mrs. Peters. "Roger could have died, or been seriously injured. He could have had brain damage."

"He does have brain damage," whispered Rachel. "He was born with it."

"The important thing here," said their leader, "is that we have learned that a bike is not a toy. Riding one means you follow the same rules as if you were driving a car. We have a lot to learn about bike safety. And that's going to be our next project. We're going to learn how to protect ourselves and others when riding bikes."

"Do we get a badge for it?" asked Lisa.

"Yes. After you all learn the safety rules, and practice them, you'll get a badge," said Mrs. Peters.

"Yay!" shouted the Pee Wees. It might

be hard work, and it might be kind of boring, but if there was a badge at the end it
would be worth it. And of course, thought
Molly, everyone wants to be safe. But
then, none of the other Pee Wees would
ride a bike down a slide. It didn't take a
lot of rules and a badge to know how
dumb and dangerous that was.

"Today I'm going to discuss bike safety
and give you all copies of the rules we
need to know," said their leader. "We'll
also learn how to take care of our bikes
and keep them in good condition. I realize
Roger isn't here, but I'll give him his own
lesson when he's better. And besides
learning and practicing the bike rules, I
have a fun project in mind to earn money
for a good deed."

The Pee Wees all paid close attention
when they heard the word *fun*. *Project*
wasn't such a good word, but *fun* was.

"I thought a good way to wind up our bike safety program would be to raise money to buy bikes for children who can't afford them. That way we can give them a bike and be sure they know the safety rules before they ride them."

"Bikes are expensive," said Kenny. "How can we earn the money?"

"We may be able to buy used bikes," said Mrs. Peters. "And some business people may donate some. We'll earn as much money as we can and buy what we can afford.

"I thought and thought about how to earn money," Mrs. Peters went on. "Then I read about a group of children in Endicott, New York, who collected recipes to make their very own cookbook. We can do the same thing. Mr. Peters can print them on his computer. In between the recipes, we'll print the bike safety rules. That way, both the parents and their children will see them. Then we'll sell the books to earn money for bikes. What do you think of that idea?"

"I don't know how to cook," said Tim. "I don't have any recipes."

"Neither do I," said Sonny. "My mom doesn't let me use the stove."

Mrs. Peters held up her hand. "You don't actually have to cook these things," she said. "You just ask your moms and dads and maybe some local restaurants for their favorite recipes. When we get enough, we'll choose the best and put them into a book."

"Can it be a French recipe?" asked Rachel. "My mom does a lot of French cooking. I know she has a great recipe for *coq au vin*, and cherries flambé."

"She always has to be different," Mary Beth whispered to Molly. "What's the matter with just plain American food?"

"That sounds wonderful, Rachel," said their leader.

"Maybe we should have a whole foreign section!" said Ashley. "Like Chinese and Mexican, and even some Thai food."

"Pooh," said Sonny. "I don't want to eat ties. And I can't read that Chinese stuff. I've got my favorite recipe right in my head. It's a hot dog on a bun with mustard and ketchup."

Molly was just going to say how silly that was—everyone knew how to make hot dogs. But Jody said, "That's my favorite recipe too. It's good to have some recipes that are easy to make and that everyone likes, along with the foreign ones."

Jody was right, of course. He always

made people feel good. Just once, thought Molly, I'd like to see him say something dumb.

"These are all great ideas," said Mrs. Peters. "We're off to a good start. While we learn about bike safety, you can begin collecting recipes that are good for both children and adults to make—some American and some from other places. We'll have to get started right away so they can be typed up on the computer and printed out. Then we'll get busy selling them and taking orders.

"And now, let's talk bike safety!"

CHAPTER 5

Signs and Signals

After the discussion about recipes and food, the Pee Wees felt hungry. So before they went over the safety rules, Mrs. Stone came downstairs with a plate of brownies. Each brownie had a tiny plastic bike on it!

"Look how cute they are!" said Rachel. "This red one is just like mine!"

The Pee Wees ate their brownies and drank their milk and raced their little bikes up and down the table. Sonny made screeching noises with his. Still, Molly thought it wasn't as noisy as it would

have been if Roger had been there. Roger was the noisiest and wildest Pee Wee of all.

"Now," said Mrs. Peters, "we'll get down to business."

Their leader passed out little red booklets with BIKE SAFETY printed in big black letters on the cover. They were from the police department. Inside were little stick figures wearing safety helmets, riding stick bikes, and obeying all the bike rules.

"The first thing to remember," said Mrs. Peters, holding up her booklet, "is that a bike rider must obey the very same laws and rules of the road as a car."

Hands began to wave. "Mrs. Peters, I can't honk like a car, I have no horn on my bike!" said Tracy.

"I don't have headlights," said Lisa.

"My bike is nothing like a car," said Tim. "It doesn't use gas and it hasn't got four wheels."

Mrs. Peters held up her hand. "But cyclists can still obey certain rules of the road," she said. "For example, when you're going to turn a corner, you have to signal, just the way people driving cars signal their turns."

Now all the Pee Wees were frowning. "We don't have signal lights!" said Patty.

"Bike signaling is done with your arm," said Mrs. Peters, "just as people in cars signaled long ago before cars had automatic signal lights. When you want to turn left, you slow down and extend your left arm out at your side."

Mrs. Peters demonstrated. Then all the Pee Wees signaled too.

"And for a right turn," she said, "you

41

put your left arm out, but you point it up." She showed them and held up the picture in the book.

"And when you stop," she went on, "you slow down and extend your left arm, pointing it down. That warns the people behind you that you're stopping."

The Pee Wees practiced signaling—right, left, and stopping.

"The next rule to remember is always to ride in the street, not on the sidewalk. Bikes on the sidewalk are dangerous to pedestrians. Also, you ride your bikes on the right side of the street, just like cars."

Hands waved. "Mrs. Peters," said Rachel, "that's not always true. If you're in England you have to drive on the left side of the road. It's a law."

Mary Beth rolled her eyes.

"That's true, Rachel," said their leader,

"but we aren't in England, we're in Minnesota."

Mrs. Peters went on. "Another thing to remember is to ride close to the curb, single file, or in the bike lane if there is one. Listen carefully for traffic, and never wear headphones while you're riding. It makes it hard to pay attention to the road. And cyclists must obey all traffic signs. Stop signs are for bike riders, and so are stoplights.

"At busy intersections, walk your bike across the street. And never ride double on one bike."

"I always ride with Rog," said Sonny. "I hang on to him. It's lots of fun, especially going down those big hills!"

Mrs. Peters frowned. "Never put two people on one bike. And that means you and Roger. If you're not ready to follow rules, you're not ready to ride a bike."

"Sonny isn't ready," whispered Mary Beth to Molly. (She whispered so that his mother wouldn't hear her.) "He just got his training wheels off his bike!"

"Next rule: You don't do stunt riding in the street," said their leader. "You ride in a straight line, with both hands on the handlebars and both wheels on the pavement."

"How can I keep both hands on the handlebars if I have to stick out my arm at the corners to signal?" asked Tim.

"You slow down, signal, then put both hands back on the bars when you turn," said Mrs. Peters.

"Boy, there are a lot of rules," said Tracy. "I hope I can remember all of them."

Molly agreed with Tracy. It wasn't easy to remember all this. And there was a lot more in the little booklet.

"Now, before you even start to ride your bike," said Mrs. Peters, "your bike must be registered and have a license."

"Mine does!" said Kevin.

"Mine too!" said Kenny.

"It must also have reflectors in the front and back, and a headlight for when you must ride at night or on foggy days. It should have a checkup every spring to be sure the brakes work. You must have a lock, park in a bike rack, and—this is very important—you *must* wear a helmet. If Roger had worn a helmet, he might not have had a concussion."

"If he hadn't gone down the slide on his bike, he wouldn't have had a concussion for sure," grumbled Rachel.

"This page," said Mrs. Peters, "has all the traffic signs and signals you need to know."

She held it up for the Pee Wees to see. Some of the signs said WAIT, DON'T WALK, ONE WAY, DON'T ENTER, KEEP RIGHT, STOP, and YIELD.

"Now, I want you to study all these signs and rules this week, and we'll have a little quiz on them later. I'll ask each of you only one question about something in this booklet, but you won't know what question it will be.

"We'll also look at all your bikes to be sure they're in good shape and safe to ride. So take these booklets home and show them to your parents. They'll want to help you get your bikes ready."

"Mine is ready now," said Rachel. "I even have reflector tape on my pedals."

"Very good, Rachel," said their leader. "So once you study your rules, you'll be free to start looking for your recipe. The sooner we get those recipes collected, the sooner we can get the books made and sold.

"And now, Mrs. Peters said, "we'll do a few exercises, since we've been sitting still a long time."

The Pee Wees stretched and did push-ups and told about their good deeds. Then they sang the Pee Wee song. It was time to go home. Home to think about bike safety!

And also about recipes. Rat's knees, where could Molly find a good recipe? Her mother's recipes were boring, like Jell-O salads and hamburger hot dish. Molly wanted something special. Something good enough to be in print. Something good enough to go into the Pee Wee bike safety cookbook with her name on it.

CHAPTER 6

Molly's Favorite Fast Recipe

"I don't like the word *quiz*," said Lisa on the way home. "It's just another word for *test*, and *test* sounds too much like school."

Tracy nodded. "Teachers say *quiz* to fool us into thinking it's a game instead of a test. But we're no fools. A test is a test."

"My mom studied a book like this when she took her driver's test," said Tim. "She passed and got her license. We don't get a driver's license for passing."

"No, but we get a badge," said Jody.

"That's just as good. Kids can't drive cars anyway. A license wouldn't do us any good. Besides, a test has lots of questions. We only have to answer one."

Jody is right, thought Molly. Jody always saw the good side of hard things. He made it all sound easy.

At the corner Mary Beth and Molly said good-bye to the others. Then they walked to Molly's house and sat down in the kitchen to talk about recipes.

"Rachel will bring one of those fancy French ones," said Mary Beth. "Maybe I'll just bring my mom's gingersnap recipe. Everybody likes those."

Molly nodded. Gingersnaps were okay. But Molly wanted something no one else would bring. She wanted a rare bird, as her grandma would say.

"Maybe I'll go to the Green Lantern and ask the cook for a recipe," said Molly. The

Green Lantern was a local restaurant where Mr. Duff took the family sometimes for special occasions like Mother's Day.

"I don't think they like to give out their recipes," said Mary Beth. "If they do that, everyone will cook the stuff at home and they won't pay to eat there."

Molly hadn't thought about that. It made sense.

"You could get a recipe from another cookbook," said her friend. "At the library."

"That's cheating," said Molly. "I can't take a recipe from another cookbook and put it in ours. I want one that isn't in any other cookbook."

"Then you'll have to make one up," said Mary Beth. "That's the only way to be sure no other book will have it."

Molly snapped her fingers. Then she stood up and clapped her hands. "That's it!'' she said. "My aunt made up a recipe when she was here! She took leftovers from the refrigerator, like ham and aspar-agus and cheese and tomatoes and onions, and put them in the frying pan. Then she put two eggs on top of everything, and salt and pepper, and mixed it all up. When it was cooked she put the whole thing on a piece of toast. It was really good!''

"Let's write it down,'' said Mary Beth. "You have to have the amounts just right.''

Before they could start writing, the doorbell rang. Molly looked out the win-dow.

"It's Roger!'' she said. "What does he want?''

She opened the door and said, "Aren't you supposed to be sick?''

"I'm okay now," he said. "Can I come in?"

Molly couldn't be rude to someone whose life she'd just saved. "I guess so," she said.

"What are you guys doing?" he asked.

Mary Beth told him about the recipes.

"We're busy," she said.

"I'll help," Roger said.

Roger wanted to help them? Molly couldn't believe it.

Suddenly an awful thought came to Molly. Roger was afraid his new bike would be stolen if he didn't repay them for saving his life! Kenny's words must have bothered him. She whispered this to Mary Beth.

"I suppose we'd better let him help us and get it over with," Mary Beth whispered back.

"You can copy the recipe on a card," said Molly to Roger. "I'll call my aunt."

She gave Roger a card and a pencil. When Molly's aunt told her the recipe on the phone, she repeated it to Roger.

Molly's aunt said the amounts didn't have to be exact. She told them that if they used two cups of veggies and meat or fish, combined with two beaten eggs, they would have enough for two big open-faced sandwiches on toast. "Big enough even for your dad!" laughed Molly's aunt. "He's a big eater, and he liked my recipe."

Molly thanked her aunt, and Roger finished writing down what she had said. He wrote down all the ingredients and the directions. At the end he wrote, "Serve on toast. Serves two or more."

"What are you going to call it?" said Mary Beth. "It has to have a name."

"I think I'll call it 'Molly's Aunt's Favorite Fast Recipe.' People like fast stuff when they come home from work and don't have much time. This won't take any time at all."

Roger wrote the name at the top. "How do you spell *favorite*?" he asked.

Molly spelled it for him.

"I'll stop at Mrs. Peters' house on my way home and give it to her," said Roger.

Before Molly could stop him, he was out the door and gone.

"What if he loses it?" cried Molly.

"He won't," said Mary Beth. "He doesn't want seven years' bad luck. And now we're through with him."

Well, that's good, Molly thought. And now one of her tasks was done! At this rate, getting the bike safety badge would be a snap.

That weekend Molly studied the bike rules. Her dad quizzed her on the signals and signs. Then they took Molly's bike into the shop to get a checkup and grease job.

"Just like our car!" said Mr. Duff. "Safety first!" He also bought Molly a brand-new purple helmet.

From there they went to the police station and got a license for the bike.

And then they stopped at Big Burger for lunch.

"Troop 23 will have the safest bikes in town!" said Mr. Duff.

"Except for Roger," said Molly, dipping her french fry in ketchup. "He comes back on Tuesday, and I'll bet he's just as mean as ever."

Molly was right. On Tuesday Roger was back at Scouts. His dad brought him in and said, "Roger would like to thank all of you, especially Molly and Mary Beth, for calling for help in time."

Molly felt embarrassed. She didn't want any thanks.

And Roger didn't give any. His father kept nudging him. He finally stood up and said, "Thanks," so softly that hardly anyone could hear him.

"Roger is a little bit shy," said Mr. White.

"Shy?" Rachel whispered to Molly. "The day Roger is shy I'll eat my hat!"

Mr. White thanked the troop for Roger. He said that if they had not acted quickly and maturely, Roger might not have been here today. Mr. White was so grateful, he got tears in his eyes. "I could have lost my only son if it had not been for the Pee Wee Scouts."

"Why would anyone want a kid like

Roger anyway?" Mary Beth whispered to Molly.

"I suppose when someone is part of your family, you don't notice what they're really like," Molly whispered back. "It's like being in love. My aunt says you can't see straight."

CHAPTER 7

Roger's Return

When Mr. White had left, Roger ran around, bragging to everyone about his concussion and showing them how big the lump on his head had been.

"He wouldn't be bragging if he was dead," said Tracy.

"My mom said next time he might not be so lucky," said Lisa.

"Roger's always lucky," scoffed Rachel. "He gets away with murder."

Roger was chasing the Peterses' dog, Lucky, around the basement. Roger seems

even wilder than before, thought Molly. Since he had repaid Molly and Mary Beth by helping with the recipe, he must think his job was done.

When Mrs. Stone asked Roger to help carry Nick's playpen downstairs, he said, "The doctor told me I can't do any lifting. My head's going to be kind of fragile for a long time. I might get dizzy and fall over and faint."

"You're right about one thing," said Rachel. "You have a fragile head. It's empty like an eggshell."

Roger stuck his tongue out at Rachel.

"Hey, you guys," he said. "You've got to see my new bike! It's a Mountain Ranger. It's got millions of gears. I get to be in a race on Sunday—all the way to Minneapolis."

"How can he race to Minneapolis, up

all those hills, if he can't lift a little thing like a playpen?" demanded Ashley.

"And why does he get a brand-new bike?" said Kevin. "He shouldn't be riding a bike at all, the way he acts."

Roger had run up the steps and was trying to drag the new bike into the house for the Pee Wees to see. Mrs. Peters ran up the steps after him and made him take it outside again.

"I'll show you guys later," said Roger.

Mrs. Peters clapped her hands for everyone to get down to business. And the business wasn't Roger. He's already taken up enough time, thought Molly.

"Now!" said their leader. "Before we talk about bike safety, tell me—have you brought your recipes?"

Molly asked Mrs. Peters if Roger had given her the recipe.

"Yes," Mrs. Peters said. "You were the first one to get yours in!"

Well, that was good news. Roger really had been a help!

Lisa, Jody, Kenny, and Tim also handed theirs in.

"My recipe has been tested," said Molly. "And it's fast."

"Good," said Mrs. Peters. "People like fast recipes when they work all day."

"Mine is fast too," said Lisa.

"Great," said Mrs. Peters. "Maybe the rest of you can bring your recipes to my house during the week. That way we can get the book put together as quickly as possible.

"And now, let's go outside and check those bikes to see if they have licenses and reflectors!"

Most of the Pee Wees were ready. Their

bikes had had checkups, and some even had new brakes.

"I washed and waxed mine," said Kenny. "And Patty's too."

Mrs. Peters admired the bikes and made check marks in a box after each of their names on her clipboard. Then they went back downstairs to start the quiz.

Instead of asking a question and then looking for someone who knew the answer, Mrs. Peters would call on a person first. *Then* she would ask that person a question. The Pee Wees all looked worried.

"Let's start with Lisa," said their leader. She looked down at the rule booklet. "What color, Lisa, should the reflectors on the bike's pedals be?"

Everyone frowned. No one remembered

about reflectors on pedals. Except Rachel. Her hand was waving.

"This question is only for Lisa," said Mrs. Peters firmly. Rachel put her hand down.

"I don't think you told us that," said Lisa.

"No, but I told you to read the booklet," said Mrs. Peters, "and that everything in it could be on the quiz."

Lisa looked as if she might cry.

Mrs. Peters held up the booklet and read, " 'Each pedal must have a white or yellow reflector on it, and it must be able to be seen for two hundred feet.' "

Molly wrote it down in her note book, even though Mrs. Peters probably wouldn't ask that same question again. Everyone would remember it now.

"I'll ask you another question next

week, Lisa," said Mrs. Peters. "Now, Molly Duff."

Molly's knees felt like Jell-O, but she stood up.

"When you come out of an alley or driveway on your bike, what do you do before entering the street?"

Molly wondered if this was a trick question. Maybe the answer was stop. But maybe it was look both ways. Maybe the rule was one of those things, maybe it was the other, or maybe it was both things! She'd have to take a chance.

"Stop and look both ways," said Molly.

"Good, Molly. That was the perfect answer! I can see you read your book!" Mrs. Peters quizzed a few more Pee Wees and then said, "I'll quiz the rest of you next week."

"You were lucky," whispered Mary Beth. "That was an easy question."

Molly didn't think it was easy! But now she had two parts of her badge done. She had passed her quiz and turned in her recipe. Things were going well. Almost too well.

CHAPTER 8

Scrambled Eggs

Mrs. Peters talked some more about kickstands and yield signs and staying away from freeways and railroad tracks. She talked about one-way streets too. Soon the meeting was over. "If everyone gets their recipes in," she told the Scouts, "we should have our cookbooks ready by our next meeting."

On the day before the next meeting, Sonny called Molly on the phone.

"Hey, your recipe was icky!" he said. "My mom got the first copy of the cookbook, and your recipe should be called 'Scrambled Eggs, Enough for an Army.' "

He hung up. Before Molly could figure out what had gone wrong, Rachel called.

"We got an advance copy of the cookbook," she said, "and my mom said I couldn't make your recipe because of all the eggs. Our skin could break out or we could get high cholesterol or something."

"It's a good recipe," said Molly. "We make it all the time."

"Well, I don't think it's healthy," said Rachel, and she hung up.

All night Molly wondered what was wrong with her aunt's recipe. It was good—it was Molly's favorite! And it was fast.

At the next meeting, Molly found out what the problem was. The cookbooks were printed and waiting for them.

"I think they're beautiful!" said Mrs. Peters. "I'll give each of you ten to sell. When you sell those, I'll give you ten more."

Sonny and Rachel were waving their hands. Molly knew what they were going to say. They both complained about Molly's recipe.

"All these recipes have been tested," said their leader. "You must have made a mistake."

"I can take forty cookbooks, Mrs. Peters," said Ashley. "My dad can put them in his office and his customers will buy them."

"Unless they're allergic to eggs," said Rachel.

"I'm allergic to eggs," said Tracy.

"Well, you'd better stay away from page nineteen, then," said Kevin. "This recipe has twenty eggs!"

Mrs. Peters and the Pee Wees turned to page nineteen.

"Rat's knees!" yelled Molly. "That's my recipe! It's supposed to be two eggs!"

Mrs. Peters ran upstairs and came down with Molly's recipe. She was frowning.

"Your recipe card says twenty, Molly. Twenty eggs."

No wonder Sonny and Rachel had complained!

Molly and Mary Beth glared at Roger. "It's your fault," said Molly, pointing at him.

"Roger wrote it down, Mrs. Peters," said Mary Beth. "I'll bet he did it on purpose!"

"Hey, I did not!" said Roger. "That's what Molly told me, twenty eggs!"

"I did not!" said Molly. "Rat's knees, I know better than to use twenty eggs!" She stamped her foot.

Mrs. Peters sighed. "The thing is," she said, "how do we correct it?"

She looked at the piles of cookbooks on the table. And on the chairs. Piles and piles of cookbooks, ready to sell. Except for one thing: piles and piles of eggs. In the wrong place!

"Well, we can't reprint all of these books," she said. "It will take too long and be too expensive. Maybe we can change the twenty to a two."

"Roger should do it," said Rachel. "It's his fault."

"He can help," said Mrs. Peters. "We'll all have to pitch in and cross off that zero."

The Pee Wees looked at all the books. "In every book?" asked Kenny.

It did seem like a huge task to Molly. Could they do it?

"We could think of it as a giant good

deed," said Jody. "If we all worked on it, it wouldn't take that long."

"Well, it looks as if that's the only thing we *can* do," said their leader. "We can all work, and while we're doing that, I can continue with my quiz."

"I think we should do something more entertaining, to make the time go faster," said Ashley. "Like tell riddles or jokes or maybe have a snack."

"Let's do both," said Mrs. Peters.

She got them all pencils and showed them how to cross out the zero on page nineteen. She showed them how to do it carefully and neatly.

"This will take forever," said Kenny. "Why was Roger helping you, anyway?"

"Because we saved his life," said Mary Beth crossly.

"Now you'll still have seven years' bad

luck, Roger," laughed Kenny. "You'll have to do something else to repay them."

Molly and Mary Beth groaned. Kenny was making things worse.

"We don't want any more help," said Molly to Roger. "Just stay away from us."

"I don't want my bike stolen," he said. "I've got to help you guys."

At first, progress with the cookbooks was slow. Then Jody had the idea that one person should open all the books to page nineteen so that they would be ready. After that, things went much faster. Before long, one whole stack of books was done. But there were still many undone stacks. Mrs. Peters read the rules while they worked and quizzed everyone who had not been quizzed last week. Then Mr. Peters came home and helped too. He told them stories and made popcorn and lemonade. Then they all sang together. By the end of the meeting, Mr. Peters said, "I think Mrs. Peters and I can finish these up tonight after Nick is in bed."

The Pee Wees stood up and stretched. Molly's fingers were stiff. "I have writer's cramp," she said. "Just like real writers get."

The stiff Pee Wees got ready to leave. "That was a giant good deed you all did today," said Mrs. Peters. "And there are enough books finished for you all to take a pile to sell. Don't go to strangers' houses, just sell in your own neighborhood and to relatives and friends."

"And my dad's dental patients," said Rachel.

All week Molly sold books. She sold them to the couple next door and to her aunt and to her mom's and dad's friends. Molly left a book near the front door so

that anyone who stopped by would see it. She put a tag on it that said, FOR SALE. HELP THE BIKE FUND.

Sure enough, the mail person and the UPS man and even the dry cleaning lady bought one. All the Scouts went back to Mrs. Peters's house for more. At their next Tuesday meeting, their leader announced that they had sold almost every book. There was plenty of money for several bikes. Along with the bikes the business-people had donated, and the bikes that had been rebuilt, the Pee Wees had twelve bikes to give to children who would not have had a bike otherwise.

"The bike committee has chosen children who need our help the most. We'll take the bikes to them along with a copy of the bike rules, and a cookbook for their parents," said Mrs. Peters.

"Next week," she continued, "We'll get

our badges. But first, we're going to take our bike hike on Saturday. It will give us a chance to put all the bike rules into practice. I'd like you all to be at my house at nine o'clock sharp, with your bikes and helmets."

"Yay!" shouted the Pee Wees.

"This is a fun badge," said Mary Beth. "At least, it is now that we know the rules and passed the quiz!"

Mary Beth is right, thought Molly. Now all there is to look forward to is pure fun and no work!

There was no cloud on the horizon. Unless you wanted to call Roger a cloud.

CHAPTER 9

Ready, Set, Ride!

Saturday morning dawned bright and clear. Molly's dad made pancakes for breakfast. "You'll need a lot of strength to do all that pedaling," he said.

When Molly got to the Peterses' house, the Pee Wees were there, along with some of the parents who were going on the trip to help out.

"Now that we all know the bike rules, and have our bikes in tip-top shape, we should have a wonderful bike hike!" said

Mrs. Peters. Baby Nick was in a safety seat behind Mr. Peters. Even Nick was wearing a helmet. A baby helmet.

"Hey, Stone, you got your training wheels off that thing?" Roger teased Sonny.

Sonny turned bright red. "I haven't had training wheels on my bike for a long time," he said.

"I don't know why Sonny wants Roger for a best friend," said Mary Beth. "Roger is so mean to him."

"All I know is, I want to stay away from Roger on this ride," said Molly. "I have a feeling he's still watching for some chance to repay us."

"Remember, now," said Mr. Peters. "Ride single file, and keep alert for cars. Stay on the edge of the road. Mrs. Peters and I will lead the troop, and there will be parents in the middle and parents at the end. If there's any trouble, we'll be close at hand."

"We have snacks in our backpacks," said Tim's mother, who was one of the chaperones, "for our break in the park. By lunchtime we should be as far as the Countryside Eatery. We'll all have lunch there."

"And we have water here in these bottles," said Tracy's father, pointing to the containers clamped onto his bike.

"We have first aid in this kit," said Mrs. Peters, holding up a box with a red cross on it. "Let's hope we don't have to use it!"

"I hope there's something in it for a concussion," said Rachel. "Who knows what Roger will do this time!" Roger made a face at Rachel.

"We can't carry a dead Pee Wee on our

bikes!" said Mary Beth. "And we can't call 911 out in the country."

"I think the Peterses have a cellular phone," said Rachel. "But it might be too late by the time help got there."

Molly hoped she wouldn't have to save Roger twice. Then he would have to repay her twice!

Troop 23 got on their bikes and followed the Peterses. They went down one block and up another toward the country road. Nearby, cars whizzed along the freeway. Trucks hummed across overpasses. Airplanes buzzed through the air, and boats sailed on the river. Everyone was out enjoying the fine day.

"My foot hurts," cried Tim when they had been riding a half hour. "I think it's bleeding."

The troop stopped, and Mrs. Noon took

a look at Tim's foot. He had a blister on his heel. It was red and sore from his sneaker rubbing against it. Mrs. Peters put some medicine on it, then covered it with a Band-Aid.

"I think that will feel better," she said. It did.

"This is the way to travel," said Jody when they were on the road again. He had a special bike with three wheels and a motor. "It's more fun than being inside a car."

"Jody never complains about anything," said Lisa. "Even though he can't walk."

"I wouldn't complain either," said Tracy, "if I had a wheelchair to ride in and a bike with a motor."

"That doesn't make up for not walking," said Mary Beth.

"It does too," said Tracy.

Molly agreed that Jody had some neat stuff. But it didn't make up for never being able to walk in your whole entire life. No matter what, Jody was someone everybody liked. He didn't hurt people's feelings the way Roger did.

"I'm tired," cried Kenny. "It's hard going up all these hills!"

"That's because you don't have a bike like mine," said Sonny. "I can just coast up the hills with my feet off the pedals."

To show everyone, Sonny put his feet up on the handlebars. His bike went up the curb and hit a bush. Off he tumbled into the hedge.

Everyone stopped while Mr. Peters and Mr. Barnes picked Sonny up out of the bush and brushed him off.

Mrs. Stone gave him a talk about stunt riding. "A bike shouldn't be used for showing off," she said.

"His mom always scolds him, but he never changes," sighed Patty.

Sonny had torn his pants and there was dirt on his shirt, but he seemed to be okay.

"I think it's time for a break," said Mrs. Noon. "Let's stop in the park and have our snack and a refreshing cup of water."

In the park there was a sandbox for baby Nick and swings for the Pee Wees.

"I can't feel my feet!" said Mary Beth when she got off her bike. None of the other Pee Wees could either. They limped and hopped and rubbed their feet until the feeling came back.

After the snacks and a quick rest, the bike hike continued.

"One good thing about bikes," laughed Mr. Peters, "is that we don't have to stop for gas!"

The Pee Wees rode up and down more hills. They stopped to talk to some cows that stood behind a fence watching the bikers. The cows chewed and watched, watched and chewed.

"All they do is eat," said Lisa.

"And then we eat them," said Roger.

The Pee Wees glared at Roger. "I think it's awful to eat animals!" said Rachel. "And to wear fur coats."

"My dad and I put these great big thick steaks on the grill all summer," said Roger, rubbing his stomach.

"Oh, gross!" said Rachel. "Eating cows should be banned!"

Mr. Peters moved the troop along before the argument could get worse.

Molly didn't know what to think. She often got mixed up about what she believed. She wouldn't want to hurt a cow, or any animal. But she didn't say no when her dad wanted to get take-out hamburgers. She sighed. Life was so confusing. She wished there were some rules that she could follow that would always be right.

"There's the Countryside Eatery!" said Jody, pointing up ahead. "We get to eat lunch!"

"I'm ready," said Mary Beth. "All that exercise has made me really hungry."

"I'm starving," said Molly. She was thinking about how good a great big juicy hamburger would taste, with ketchup and mustard and onions and tomato.

But then she thought of the cows' faces and knew it would be a hard thing to order.

CHAPTER 10

Roger to the Rescue

There were bike racks in front of the restaurant.

"They must have known we were coming!" said Mrs. Noon.

The Pee Wees neatly parked and locked their bikes in the racks. Molly had a hard time getting her lock to snap shut.

Some of the Pee Wees had hamburgers (Roger had two) and some had pizza. Molly had a veggie burger and french fries.

"Hey, I want a great big sundae for dessert!" said Roger. "With gallons of hot fudge!"

"Your teeth are going to fall out," said Rachel.

"Then I'll get false ones like my dad," said Roger.

It turned out all the Pee Wees wanted ice cream—but not gallons of hot fudge. As they ate, they looked out the window at the people coming and going in cars and on bikes.

All of a sudden Roger left his hot fudge, got up, and dashed out the door. As the Pee Wees watched, he ran to the bike rack. A boy was there taking a bike from the rack. Roger stopped him. The Pee Wees couldn't hear what they were saying, but they could see they were arguing.

"Now what kind of trouble is Roger in?" sighed Mrs. Stone.

Roger had grabbed the bike and was pushing the boy away.

"Roger won't let that boy take his own bike!" said Kenny. "Look, he's picking a fight with that kid!"

"That's not his own bike!" said Molly suddenly. "That's *my* bike!"

The boy ran off, and Roger put Molly's bike back in the rack. He carefully clamped the lock shut. When he came in, Roger yelled, "Hey, Duff, how come your bike wasn't locked up?"

Molly said, "I couldn't get the lock closed tight."

"I'll show you how to do it," said Roger. "You have to turn it a certain way before you snap it. That kid was taking your bike. He said he thought it was his."

Molly felt like running up and hugging Roger to thank him for saving her bike! Of

all people! Roger actually had done something nice!

Mrs. Peters patted Roger on the back and congratulated him for his good deed.

"It was nothing," said Roger. "Those locks are hard to close. It wasn't Molly's fault."

Molly thanked Roger—without hugging him—and wondered why someone would try to steal her bike.

"I think he saw it was the only bike that was unlocked," said Roger, as if he knew what she had been thinking.

"Well, all's well that ends well," said Mrs. Noon. "We were all lucky today."

"We had a good lunch, and now it's time to start for home!" said their leader.

Roger showed Molly how to lock and unlock her bike easily. Then everyone set off, going up the hills they'd gone down, and down the hills they'd gone up. They stopped in the park again to rest. By the time they got home, everyone was very, very tired.

"I want to sleep for a week!" said Molly.

"You can't," said Mrs. Peters. "Tomorrow is badge day!"

And it was. After a good night's sleep, every Pee Wee went to Mrs. Peters's house and got a badge with a bright red bike on it.

Then they all went to the police station. The bike committee gave out the bikes they had purchased with their cookbook money. The new bike owners seemed happy and excited. They thanked the Pee Wees and their leaders.

The police registered the new bikes, and the new owners studied the bike rules.

"We have to hand it to Molly and Mary Beth for starting all this pedal power by

calling 911 and getting help for Roger," said Mrs. Peters. "It was the reason for our bike safety program, and our cookbooks, and our new badges."

"And we have to hand it to Roger for saving Molly's bike," laughed Mr. Peters.

"Now we're even," said Molly. "Roger repaid us, so he doesn't have to do anything else nice for us. And he won't have seven years of bad luck!"

"Hey!" said Roger. "That's right! We're even! I didn't even realize I was repaying you!"

"I'll bet that's the only real good deed Roger ever did in his life!" laughed Mary Beth. "And there wasn't even anything in it for him! Or at least, he forgot that there was!"

The new bike owners joined the Pee Wees in singing the Pee Wee song and saying the Pee Wee pledge. And then it was time to go.

"Mrs. Peters, what badge are we going to earn next?" asked Ashley.

Mrs. Peters laughed. "Let's not talk about that yet," she said. "Let's have a good rest first."

But the Pee Wees never wanted a rest from new badges.

Rat's knees, thought Molly. That's what Pee Wee Scouts is all about!

Pee Wee Scout Song
(to the tune of
"Old MacDonald Had a Farm")

Scouts are helpers, Scouts have fun
Pee Wee, Pee Wee Scouts!
We sing and play when work is done,
Pee Wee, Pee Wee Scouts!

With a good deed here,
And an errand there,
Here a hand, there a hand,
Everywhere a good hand.

Scouts are helpers, Scouts have fun,
Pee Wee, Pee Wee Scouts!

Pee Wee Scout Pledge

We love our country
And our home,
Our school and neighbors too.

As Pee Wee Scouts
We pledge our best
In everything we do.